THE GIRL AT
THE RIVER

To Sis
Gerry
From Sis
Tangie
May This Book
Bless Your Life

The Girl at the River

The River

Blindsided by Darkness and Deception

Tangerlene Francis

Library of Congress Control Number:		2018900147
ISBN:	Hardcover	978-1-5434-7674-3
	Softcover	978-1-5434-7673-6
	eBook	978-1-5434-7672-9

Print information available on the last page.

Rev. date: 02/09/2018

To order additional copies of this book, contact:
tangerlenefrancis.com
Xlibris
1-888-795-4274
www.Xlibris.com
Orders@Xlibris.com
772532

CONTENTS

DEDICATION

I would like to dedicate this book to my angel, Jasmine Hines. I nurtured and loved you while in my womb, as a child and now a young adult. I've watched you mature into an intelligent young woman full of wisdom beyond your years. I thank God for the river in your life and pray that you will continue to transition into the woman that God has called you to be. You're not perfect, but you are perfect for me!

Love,

Mom

CHAPTER 1

LIFE IS NOT A FAIRYTALE

A Bend in the Road Can Change Everything

Shelby, the youngest of six, grew up with her parents and siblings in Baltimore, Maryland. Her parents went through hardships trying to raise their children. Shelby's mother was a stay-at-home mom while her father worked as a factory worker. Lack of resources became a huge problem for the Clarks; they begin to quarrel daily over bills and how they would get paid.

The children would see and hear the frustration, which led to Shelby's oldest brother, Matthew, taking matters into his own hands. He began selling drugs; he was tired of kids making fun of him and his siblings for wearing old and beat-up clothing. Matthew also believed he would take some of the slack off his parents by bringing money in the home. His parents believed he had a job; however, unbeknownst to them, Matthew was making money illegally. Shelby suspected he was selling drugs because he started buying clothes she knew her parents couldn't afford. After finding stacks of money in his room, Shelby confronted Matthew. At first, he denied it but later confessed, saying he doesn't want the family to struggle anymore. While Shelby understood that part, she was afraid and expressed to him the danger of selling drugs. Matthew said, "I will be fine.

Just say a prayer for me, and promise you will not tell anyone." She agreed but decided to share this with her best friend, Mariah, who encouraged her to tell her parents, but Shelby refused.

Excited about her son graduating from high school, Mrs. Clark started planning a party to celebrate his accomplishment when she received a call that Matthew had been murdered. Needless to say, this was devastating news and left a huge void in the Clark family. Shelby was distraught; she blamed herself and was filled with guilt, so much so she attempted to commit suicide but was rescued by Mariah.

After being released from the hospital, she decided to tell her parents everything she knew. Her father held resentment toward her, feeling if she had spoken up about what she knew, it could have prevented Matthew's death. The tragedy of Matthew turned their whole family around; instead of bickering over monthly bills, their focus became to heal their broken hearts. The Clarks experienced a great deal of shame and guilt surrounding Matthew's death; however, when they refused to listen to the negative voices speaking in their ears, they began to experience peace. The truth is the Clarks did everything possible to raise their children with faith, morals, and respect, yet they found themselves filled with guilt. It was their faith and river experience that gave them hope for tomorrow, but still, the Clarks would never be the same!

Eight years later...

Mourning the loss of Matthew was a huge pill to swallow; somehow... their faith, love, and support from others was able to sustain them and prevent them from drowning. Mr. and Mrs. Clark found comfort in sharing their experience with others; to them, it helped keep Matthew's memory alive. Together, they visit local schools to talk to young men and women about Matthew's death and their experience as parents.

Shelby, now a college student, plans to follow in her sister's footsteps as a nurse. She has a 4.0 GPA, and despite her school schedule, she still finds time to serve in her community. After the death of her brother, her parents formed an organization for parents of murdered children. Shelby diligently works alongside her parents to help heal and comfort her family and those who are grieving in their community. Once a month, the Clark family prepares a meal and serves it on the street to less fortunate people. They can relate to this because there was once a time when they struggled to make ends meet and were in a similar situation.

Her parents are well loved and liked in their community, but somehow, a group of girls befriend Shelby and later turn her life upside down. Shelby is a vibrant, caring young lady yet curious. She has always felt sheltered from the outside world because she is always in the books, actively involved in church and community events with her parents. Shelby's parents are devout Christians who believe true success only happens with a relationship with God. They have done everything humanly possible to instill this into Shelby's life. Her spiritual foundation revolves around the river. The river is her first love and the place that fulfills every aspect of her life.

Reflection

The Clarks encountered a storm that ripped there family in half; however, they were able to rely on their faith to get through the darkest hour in their life.

What did you learn from this chapter?

Secrets destroy family ties and causes
resentment

Are you at peace with the bend in your road?

Identify your river and its meaning?

Reflection Notes

Reflection Notes

CHAPTER 2

THE TURN

Walking into a Desert

Shelby began to associate herself with a group of college students that lived on the wild side. These girls worked hard but partied harder. They all went out for breakfast one morning and decided to gang up on Shelby, telling her she need to live a little and stop being so consumed with books, education, church, and charity events with her parents. Shelby pondered on their conservation and started to feel like she's missing out on a life full of fun. Her strong desire to test the waters will soon lead to a life-changing event. She had daily conversations with her newfound SB girls and was more convinced and curious about the lifestyle they lived. Even though they all were in college, the SB girls had great-paying jobs; in fact, they all bragged about their bank account status, the cars they drove, and the many men they dated which brought music to Shelby's ears. Shelby thought, *Wow, they have it all*; little did she know she was being deceived. She was visually impaired and couldn't see past the glitz and glimmer.

Shelby had a chat with Mariah about the girls; she invited her to meet them. Somehow, Mariah was not convinced these girls were true friends.

"Something is off with them," she told Shelby. "You better watch yourself around those girls. They are up to no good."

"Stop it! You are being silly and stuck up, then again, I think you are jealous of them."

"OK, Shelby, whatever you say. Just remember I warned you."

Stressed out, Shelby headed to the river to relax, clear her mind, and to think about her life and where it's headed. While at the river, Chelsea called to discuss some issues the SB girls were experiencing related to men. Shelby was a little reluctant because she didn't have a man in her life; however, she left the River and headed in town to meet up with the girls to chat further about the situation. In talking, she discovered all of them are involved with married men; she's no relationship expert, but Shelby knew this was wrong and not a normal relationship. Her parents taught her to value who she is as a woman, which meant to love herself enough not to share herself with a man who has another woman. Shelby's parents taught her the value in loving God, herself, and preparing for a husband, not a fling and certainly not a one-night stand. Shelby decided to share her values with the girls and the importance of loving themselves enough to wait for the man of their dreams versus the man of a fantasy.

Shelby said, "Girls, do you realize you are a spare tire to these men you are seeing? They only use you when it's a need. Spare tires are never used permanently. This is what happens when you devalue who you are."

The girls laughed.

Chelsea said, "Enough of all this boujee talk. Sweetie, we don't live in a perfect world like you. Let's talk about the party tonight. Are you down?"

The conversation was short-lived; they accused Shelby of being a snooty brat and told her she had a boring life that no one wanted. Their goal was to deter Shelby from her morals. Shelby became depressed and wondered if what the SB girls were saying had some truth to it.

She headed to the river, hoping to find peace. While at the river, Shelby received a call from one of the girls telling her the party location along with the new time change, which meant she must leave the river. She drifted away from the river without realizing it; the gradual change in her lifestyle and trips to the river caused a roadblock in her sight. Shelby couldn't see the road ahead!

Shelby headed home to prepare for a night on the town with the (SB) girls; meanwhile, her friend-enemies were plotting on how to destroy her reputation.

She had become really distracted to the point her grades have dropped drastically; she no longer attended charity events or was active in church. Shelby had not realized how much the night life affected her until she received a letter from the school, stating she received an academic dismissal because of poor achievement and performance. At that point, Shelby was really frustrated and headed to the river to pray and clear her head. Shelby decided to tell her parents the news about school. Her parents were very disappointed; however, they pointed Shelby back to the direction of God. Shelby's mother began praying over and encouraging her. Shelby lost hope of her faith and future. Although her life was surrounded by the river and it was her solid foundation, once she met the girls, that all changed. Shelby would visit the river only when she was sad, depressed, or had a problem. Shelby became distracted, deterred, and discouraged, which caused her to become unfocused.

Shelby called Mariah to invite her to a masquerade party with the SB girls. Mariah told her under no circumstances would she go anywhere with the SB girls because she did not trust them. She begged Shelby not to go; the two got into a heated argument where Shelby said some things she would later regret. After the argument, Shelby had second thoughts about going to the party. She decided to take a walk to the river to clear her head, which for her, meant prayer and meditation. She typically spent hours at the river but lately had been distracted with the girls and their drama.

Bored at home, feeling like she's missing out on something, she decided to get dressed and meet them at the party. The SB girls decided this would be the night to make their move. They planned to put something in Shelby's drink to loosen her up. Once at the party, they began to dance, mingle, and have lots of fun. Shelby thought, *Boy, have I been missing out on living the life.* Soon after, some guys approached the girls and asked if they wanted to go to a private room to smoke some weed. The girls were down for it, but Shelby was hesitant. She said, "Guys, I don't smoke."

They said, "Girl, lose up a bit and have some fun. A little smoke won't harm you."

She said no.

They said, "Well, at least have a drink."

She said okay. Shortly after drinking her drink, she passed out, and four guys took turns having sex with her. The girls left shortly after recording what they felt was a prank. When Shelby woke up, she was in bed with one of the guys. Frightened, confused, and angry, Shelby attempted to leave, but he started to beat her repeatedly.

Reflection

Shelby could not see that the SB girls were taking her on a spiral path. Her life turned from the river to the desert. She could not see the dry place she is in right now. Once she abandoned the river, things became very foggy. The warning signs were there, but Shelby ignored them because she wanted to be accepted.

What did you learn from this chapter?

_____

_____

_____

_____

How do you relate to the turn?

_____

_____

_____

_____

What is your desert?

_____

_____

_____

_____

Reflection Notes

Reflection Notes

CHAPTER 3

TRAIN WRECK

Choices + Decision = Consequences

She was finally able to escape; she jumped in her car and began driving at a high rate of speed. She lost control of her car and hit a pole. When paramedics arrived, she was unconscious; by the time she reached the hospital, she had slipped into a coma.

Shelby's parents were notified and, of course, were distraught but hopeful. They began to pray, but it seemed like the more they prayed, the worse her condition got. The doctors told Shelby's parents she had an enormous amount of trauma to her brain and chances of her regaining her life was almost impossible. The doctors instructed her parents to prepare for the worst.

In disbelief, Shelby's parents began asking questions, like how did their daughter end up on a dark wooded road and why was she driving her car naked with only a shirt. Desperate for answers, her parents went to Chelsea's house to obtain details from all the girls. One by one, they gave similar but slightly varied versions of the stories which made Shelby's parents suspicious. They proceeded to the police station to share their feelings with the police; meanwhile, the girls paid a visit to Shelby. When they saw her condition, they were saddened and felt guilty for the moment; however, they all vowed not to disclose the truth to anyone.

Chelsea just couldn't get this out of her mind; the guilt began to eat her up, so she decided to share the real story with her parents. Chelsea's parents encouraged her to tell the truth; meanwhile, Shelby's parents continued to search for answers. Chelsea and her parents decided to pay a visit to Shelby's parents. Once the truth was told, Shelby's mom became very angry and bitter toward Chelsea. She was soon reminded of her love for God and the poison anger can cause if not dealt with.

Shelby's parents began to pray with Chelsea and her parents, which opened the door for the family to hear about Jesus Christ. As they were leaving the home, Shelby's parents received a call telling them to get to the hospital right away. When they arrived, they walked in the room, and Shelby's eyes were open. When she saw her parents, tears began rolling down her face. She looked to the right and saw Chelsea and just stared at her without blinking. Chelsea walked over to her bedside and said, "I'm so sorry, Shelby. Please forgive me."

Shelby extended her hand and held Chelsea's hand really tight and nodded her head, letting her know she forgave her. In that moment, a true friendship was formed. Chelsea's coming forth with the truth diminished her relationship with the other girls. Chelsea was brave to take responsibility for her actions and reveal the truth.

Shelby had to overcome yet another tragedy in her life. After the death of her brother, she thought her family would never recover; now, she felt she screwed up again. Shelby was blind and didn't want to see the truth. The SB girls were filled with poison and were determined to spread it. They had one plan and one purpose: to destroy Shelby and hide their true identity.

In Chelsea's eyes, nothing else mattered but the truth. Although she was a willing participant in the PPAD (Party Plan and Destroy), her conscience would not allow her to act as if nothing happened like the other girls. She had nightmares about that night and decided to seek professional help.

The police were not notified of the girl's role because Shelby knew if she mentioned them, Chelsea would go down as well. She valued Chelsea's honesty and displayed true forgiveness. Shelby's mother wasn't the happiest about not moving forward with notifying the police; however, she respected her daughter's wishes and understood the reason behind it all.

The girls couldn't understand why the police never contacted them. They scratched their heads, trying to figure out what was going on. They tried to deceive Chelsea, hoping she would provide them with information, but Chelsea knew their intent; therefore, she refused to have anything to do with them.

The SB girls didn't have any restraints in life which made them a target for danger. They would soon learn the message: "If you play with fire, you will get burned."

Reflection

In the blink of an eye, Shelby's life changed forever. It wasn't the choices that caused the train wreck; it was her decisions. In life, there are boatloads of choices; it's the decisions one makes that determine the consequence.

What did you learn from this chapter?

_____

_____

_____

_____

Identify anything or any person that has the potential to cause a train wreck in your life?

_____

_____

_____

_____

Examine your life; picture yourself on a train. Are you headed in the right direction; if not, jump off now and proceed in the opposite direction before it's too late.

(What steps will you take to avoid a train wreck?)

_____

_____

_____

_____

If you are going in the right direction, make sure those on board with you are not trying to cause you to detour.

(Take inventory of those that will help you reach your destination.)

_____

_____

_____

_____

Reflection Notes

Reflection Notes

CHAPTER 4

The Hidden Truth

Living in the Shadow of Darkness

The SB girls never wanted the truth to be revealed because they wanted to maintain their image. In fact, they all blocked it out of their mind as if that night didn't exist. In the girls' eyes, it seemed realistic to hide the truth because they were not ready to face the destruction they caused.

Once Shelby told them she was a virgin, they started plotting to destroy her; without admitting it, they all were jealous and resented her. The root of the matter was the SB girls lived in the shadow of darkness from their childhood pain. As a result, it destroyed and affected the lives of many; without remorse or regret, they refused to change and took pleasure in their actions.

The SB girls wanted Shelby to believe they were all the golden girls; truth was, they were on a hunt to sabotage and pull Shelby into their darkness. Shelby lay in her hospital bed, thinking of the true message behind this nightmare. She finally realized the root of her pain was not embracing who she was; instead, she tried to fit in and be accepted by a group of girls headed for destruction.

Shelby started to ponder on their life and wanted to help them. She developed a sense of compassion and sorrow. Shelby now desired them to be free from their life of trickery. Her new outlook on life was to unmask every area in her life which would lead to helping others. Although Shelby had this desire, she didn't know how it could happen, especially since the girls were very stubborn and self-righteous.

Shelby sent a letter asking if they would visit her. She wanted to let the SB girls know she had forgiven them and hoped to persuade them to give up their lifestyle of darkness. To her surprise, they never responded; in fact, once they received the letter, they laughed and dismissed her invitation.

Chelsea lost what she thought was a friendship but gained a treasure that would last a lifetime. The girls went on with life and continued partying and causing havoc in the lives of others. They continued sleeping with married men and destroying relationships. One night, the girls had a sleepover and began gloating to each other about their actions. Although they were gloating, they all became very serious about why they took pleasure in destroying others' lives, especially men. It was at that time they all revealed they were sexually assaulted at a young age. One by one, they shared the need to control men and not let men control them.

To them, it was easier to continue their ratchet behaviors instead of seeking counseling and dealing with their pain head on. On the outside, it appeared the SB girls had it all together, but the reality was the girls had a deep wound that needed to be healed.

After their sleepover, they decided to go on a girl's trip to Virginia Beach for seven days. While there, of course, they did much drinking and partying; the last night, they decided to go on a party bus with some guys they met. The girls didn't realize the guys were connected to a sex trafficking organization.

When the girls didn't return home as planned, their parents panicked. They all notified the police and filed a missing person's report. The search for the girls began at the hotel where they stayed and concluded at the beach where three cell phones were found. The SB girls never returned and were never found.

Reflection

It would have been a great benefit for the SB girls to seek help, but denial and pride prevented them from doing such. Searching the soul is not easy; however, it releases the mind to be free and allow the open wounds to be healed. When you bury pain, it cannot be put to death until you dig it up from the root.

What did you learn from this chapter?

_____

_____

_____

_____

Do you have any wounds that need to be healed?

_____

_____

_____

_____

Can you identify your SBs (stumbling blocks)?

_____

_____

_____

_____

Reflection Notes

Reflection Notes

CHAPTER 5

SET ME FREE

The Yielding Moment

Although Shelby came out of the coma, she still had a long way to go. She was partially paralyzed; however, doctors were now hopeful that through surgery and physical therapy, there was a good chance Shelby would fully recover. This experience had tested her faith; despite the challenges, she was grateful to be alive and hoped to have a normal life again. Lying in the hospital bed, Shelby began crying out to God to heal and forgive her. It was at that moment that Shelby realized the hurt she caused her parents and best friend, Mariah. At that point, she sent a message requesting to see Mariah to ask for forgiveness. Although Shelby initiated the visit, Mariah had already forgiven Shelby and was just grateful her friend was still alive. God spared Shelby's life; she didn't want to focus on her mistakes or regrets but rather focused on Shelby getting well.

Shelby started replaying in her mind how something like this could happen. She came to realize her decisions had consequences that changed her life forever. Filled with shame, regret, and guilt, she must now rely on the foundation of her faith to put her life back together. It was Mariah who encouraged her not to condemn herself but to embrace her life that was spared.

In hanging out with the SB girls, Shelby never had time to study or visit the river, and when she did, they would always interrupt her, which caused her to leave and never return. In her yielding moment, she realized the SB girls was a huge distraction and caused a detour in her road to success. She had to take responsibility for allowing the distraction and separation from the river.

Shelby began to journal her thoughts, hoping to find peace in the midst of darkness. She had one desire: to return to the river of her life. She often reflected on the sounds of the streams while at the river. Seeing the river was one thing, but her ability to hear was most important. Once Shelby met up with the SB girls, she lost focus of her lifeline (the river), which caused her ears to clog, leaving her incapable of hearing the beautiful sound of the river.

Shelby began physical therapy which was difficult in the beginning, so much so she began to wonder if she would ever walk again; however, she was reminded of her favorite scripture, Philippians 4:13: "I can do all things through Christ who strengthens me." Shelby began to recite this scripture daily, which gave her the strength and courage to withstand therapy. After two months of intense therapy, she regained full feeling in her legs and was able to take steps on her own, which gave her joy. Shelby was overjoyed and looking forward to getting her life back on track. She planned to enroll back in school once she fully recovered; however, she received news from her doctors that changed her plans completely.

Blood test revealed Shelby was pregnant. This was devastating news, especially because of the circumstances surrounding this pregnancy. Before being raped, Shelby was a virgin and was saving herself for the man of her dreams. Suddenly, her dreams were snatched away. Hearing this news saturated any thoughts of a happy ending and sent her on an emotional rollercoaster. At that moment, she felt like a ton of bricks had fallen on her.

Shelby did not believe in abortions which left her with two options: give the child up for adoption or raise the child on her own. After much prayer, she decided to raise the child, which would be difficult to do alone. She had no idea who the father was! After seeking counseling, Shelby began preparing herself mentally to become a mother while still healing and learning how to walk.

Shelby was often haunted by that night and how it changed her life. If only she could turn back the clock and do things differently. Instead, the clock will move forward, and she must face the reality of her new life as a single mother.

Her desire to live had everything to do with her foundation of the river. Shelby had to return to the place that gave her hope, shelter, comfort, and peace. The river was that inner place that could take away all her fears, doubt, and shame. The place she longed to be, to set her free.

Reflection

The moment Shelby realized her life was in shambles; she cried out for help. Don't ever allow pride, shame, or guilt to prohibit a chance to be free. Yielding to freedom is the most powerful aspect of one's life. Seems like Shelby was hit with turbulence after turbulence but still had the desire to yield.

What have you learned from this chapter?

_____

_____

_____

_____

Can you identify any area in your life you need to be free from?

_____

_____

_____

_____

Examine your life to determine if there is need for a yield!

_____

_____

_____

_____

Reflection Notes

Reflection Notes

CHAPTER 6

Revived

From Dark to Light

After six long months, Shelby recovered completely; she was released from rehab and moved back home with her parents who would help her with the baby.

She later established a nonprofit organization for rape victims, which led into her giving charity events. At her first charity event, a gentleman walked up and presented a check for 20,000. Shelby was very astonished yet grateful. The gentleman introduced himself as John Welkmans and told Shelby the event was very important and dear to his heart. He gave her his business card and asked if the two could have lunch. She respectfully declined lunch but allowed Mr. Welkmans to share his ideas, which were impressive, for the next charity event. Two months later, she saw him at her church; he walked up to her and introduced himself. Shelby replied, "I know who you are." He laughed and asked when was the next charity event and was hoping to have lunch to exchange more ideas for the next event. She said everything would be on hold until she had the baby but did agree to contact him once she became available.

The two began connecting and sharing ideas on a regular basis. John saw that Shelby was very pregnant and didn't want to impose or disrespect her relationship with her husband by talking and sharing ideas. He was very thoughtful and wanted to meet her husband out of respect. Shelby then informed him she was not married and did not have a man in her life. Certainly, this didn't make sense to John because of her huge belly; nevertheless, John kept quiet.

Close to delivery, Shelby started feeling sad, confused, and overwhelmed. She felt alone and began to shelter herself from everyone. Meanwhile, Mariah began planning a surprise baby shower for Shelby, which turned out to be a disaster. Shelby never showed up; her parents couldn't get her out of the house. She suffered from depression and felt ashamed, which caused her to lock herself in the house.

John began thinking about Shelby often and secretly developed a strong interest in her, despite her being with child. He hoped to see her at church; however, week after week, his hope failed when she didn't show up. Finally, the church announced Shelby had given birth to a healthy baby girl named Miracle. John wanted to run to her rescue, but he didn't want to impose and overstep his boundaries. John came up with a brilliant idea; he sent her flowers, chocolate-covered strawberries, and a teddy bear for the baby. She was surprised to receive the gift; however, she decided not to call and thank him until she was released from the hospital, which left John puzzled. John shared how much he had been worried about Shelby and the baby. Shelby had doubts if what he was saying was true, but she listened. He told her he didn't need to see or talk to her every day, he just wanted to make sure she's okay.

He asked if he could e-mail her daily to check on her and the baby. She was skeptical but agreed. John began sending daily scripture to Shelby, which began to encourage and give her hope. The two began having Bible study daily via e-mail. This sparked a fire within the two of them. Shelby and John began courting over e-mail, which led to a once-a-week phone call. They dated for six months before John asked Shelby for her hand in marriage. She accepted his proposal; six months later, the two were married.

Having the baby and now a new wife, Shelby had not had the chance to do any charity events. She expressed to John the desire to plan an event soon. While they were exchanging ideas, Shelby asked him what led to his interest in charity events, particularly rape victims. Shelby began to ponder why he was so involved in this charity event particularly because he was a man. He began to share that he was hanging with the wrong crowd, went out to a party, and raped a young woman. He explained in detail how they had put a date rape pill in the lady's drink, and one by one, they began having sex with her. She looked in his eyes and burst into tears. She said, "This sounds like my story."

He asked, "Is Miracle the result of a rape?"

She nodded, and she began asking him details about that night, based on the information he provided Shelby was convinced John was one of the guys who raped her.

He begged for her forgiveness and shared how that night changed his life. He explained the void of having a father in his life left him angry and bitter. When his mother committed suicide, he felt he had nothing to live for, so he started partying, drinking, and smoking, hoping the pain would disappear. He told Shelby his pain didn't disappear; it only transferred to others.

The initial shock left Shelby angry and resentful, but Shelby was reminded of the scripture, (Matthew 6:15) "If you forgive other people when they sin against you, your heavenly Father will also forgive you." Although this was not an easy pill to swallow, Shelby was willing to begin the process of forgiveness; meanwhile, Shelby had one thought in her mind: could John be Miracle's father? The two agreed to take a paternity test, which later determined John to be the father. Shelby explained to her parents the details about John, which didn't seem to make a difference. They were angry and wanted to see John in jail. Filing charges and jail were the furthest things from Shelby's mind.

Shelby met up with Mariah for lunch to discuss John; Mariah was not thrilled to hear the news but was supportive and understood if Shelby decided to stay married to John. Shelby was distraught; she believed her life was headed in the right direction when she was hit with more devastating news. The man she vowed to spend the rest of her life with turned out to be the one that almost destroyed her life. Shelby was happy to know the missing piece to the puzzle of Miracle's father was complete. Regardless of the circumstance, Miracle would grow up knowing who her father is.

Shelby and John began counseling sessions, which appeared to help with the forgiveness portion; however, Shelby didn't feel she can stay married to John. She felt violated and did not believe she can ever look at him the same. John begged and pleaded to Shelby not to give up on their marriage.

John was hopeful their marriage could be saved if only Shelby could forgive him. In his mind, he didn't want one night of wrong to cause him to lose the love of his life.

It was very overwhelming for Shelby. She loved John and wanted to keep their family together; however, she could not get what John had done out of her mind. She went to counseling, prayed, and did everything possible to save her marriage but could not shake the feeling that John was somewhat responsible for turning her life upside down.

After one year of counseling, Shelby filed for divorce. John and Shelby are now co-parenting Miracle. John has not given up; he still believes that one day, he will be reunited with his family.

Despite everything Shelby endured, she decided to make her journey complete by stepping in the Jordan River. No longer was she bound with fear, guilt, shame, and acceptance. The moment had come for Shelby to receive her promise. Shelby went from pain to promise.

Revelation 22:2 KJV

In the midst of the street of it, and on either side of the river, was there the tree of life, which bare twelve manner of fruits, and yielded her fruit every month: and the leaves of the tree were for the healing of the nations.

Reflection

Although it may appear Shelby had the perfect life, life was far from peaches and cream. She experienced loss, pain, guilt, and shame yet was able to survive. Shelby learned a valuable lesson from her past and was able to embrace a new beginning; however, it required her to shift from a dark place. The shift allowed her to see the lighted path designed for her to follow.

What did you learn from this chapter?

_____

_____

_____

_____

Is there anything in your life that needs to be revived?

_____

_____

_____

_____

Is there anyone you need to forgive?

_____

_____

_____

_____

Reflection Notes

Reflection Notes

To My Readers

Shelby was blindsided by darkness and deception, but the reality is many people in today's society can identify with these double D's. Darkness and deception do not prefer any gender; they can land on anyone's street if they are not alert. The pair comes in many different forms but have the same purpose: to destroy you.

Blindsided moments can occur at any time; however, they are most likely to occur when one is in a defenseless state. Always safeguard your heart especially when vulnerable. Safeguarding makes you see clearly and avoid cloudy vision (CV). CV is when a person makes decisions based on impulse, emotions, or feelings. It can cause bondage and destruction in one's life, sending them on a spiral path. Oftentimes, cloudy vision is caused by some sort of hidden pain. In many cases, pain is the root cause of a person's deception of others.

If you think darkness and deception can only come from others, you're wrong! Sometimes, we deceive ourselves into believing our life is fiction. The problem is life is not a made-up story with invented characters and a plot; it's real! Life is about being honest with yourself, dealing with experiences that have caused you pain and walking in the purpose that you were created for.

Above all else, guard your heart, for everything you do flows from it. —Psalm 4:23

Reflection

Search your soul and identify any area in your life prone to the double D's before they destroy your life!

Don't allow false identities to take root in your life!

There are many false identities; listed below are some you may identify. How can you relate to these?

Image

_____

_____

_____

_____

Religion

_____

_____

_____

_____

Family

_____

_____

_____

_____

Relationships

_____

_____

_____

_____

Money

_____

_____

_____

_____

Greed

_____

_____

_____

_____

Pride

_____

_____

_____

_____

Lust

_____

_____

_____

_____

Career

_____

_____

_____

_____

Acceptance

_____

_____

_____

_____

Compromise

_____

_____

_____

_____

Addiction

_____

_____

_____

_____

Entitlement

_____

_____

_____

_____

Fill in the Blank

_____

_____

_____

_____

Reflection Notes

Reflection Notes